I Can Read!

SHARED
My First
READING

Chicken Said, "Cluck!"

by Judyann Ackerman Grant
pictures by Sue Truesdell

HarperCollins*Publishers*

HarperCollins®, 🐚®, and I Can Read Book® are trademarks of HarperCollins Publishers Inc.

www.icanread.com

Library of Congress Cataloging-in-Publication Data is available.
ISBN 978-0-06-028723-8 (trade bdg.) — ISBN 978-0-06-028724-5 (lib. bdg.)

09 10 11 12 13   LP/WOR   10 9 8   ❖   First Edition

To R.V.A., my Mom,
who instilled in me a love of reading
—J.A.G.

For Anne
—S.T.

"I will grow a pumpkin,"
said Earl.

"I will grow two pumpkins,"
said Pearl.

Chicken scratched the dirt.

"Shoo!" said Earl.

"Shoo! Shoo!" said Pearl.

"Cluck! Cluck! Cluck!"
said Chicken.

Earl dug the garden.

Pearl planted the seeds.

Chicken scratched the dirt.
"Shoo!" said Earl.

"Shoo! Shoo!" said Pearl.
"Cluck! Cluck! Cluck!"
said Chicken.

Earl watered the seeds.

Pearl pulled the weeds.

Chicken scratched the dirt.
"Shoo!" said Earl.

"Shoo! Shoo!" said Pearl.
"Cluck! Cluck! Cluck!"
said Chicken.

Earl's pumpkin grew.

Pearl's pumpkins grew.

Chicken scratched the dirt.

"Shoo!" said Earl.

"Shoo! Shoo!" said Pearl.

"Cluck! Cluck! Cluck!"
said Chicken.

Then one day
grasshoppers came.

Jump! In the garden.

Nibble.

Jump! On the pumpkins.

Nibble. Nibble.

Jump! Jump! Jump!

Nibble. Nibble. Nibble.

"Shoo!" said Earl.

"Shoo! Shoo!" said Pearl.

The grasshoppers stayed.

Chicken said, "Cluck!"
One grasshopper jumped.

Chicken said,

"Cluck! Cluck!"

Two grasshoppers jumped.

Chicken said,
"Cluck! Cluck! Cluck!"
Jump! Jump! Jump!

"Hooray!" said Earl.

"Hooray! Hooray!" said Pearl.

"Cluck! Cluck! Cluck!"
said Chicken.

29

Earl gave Chicken
one pumpkin.

Pearl gave Chicken
two pumpkins.

31

Chicken scratched the dirt.